On Monday, she checks her chair and sets it up for stunts.

Stunt Star

Written by
Cath Jones

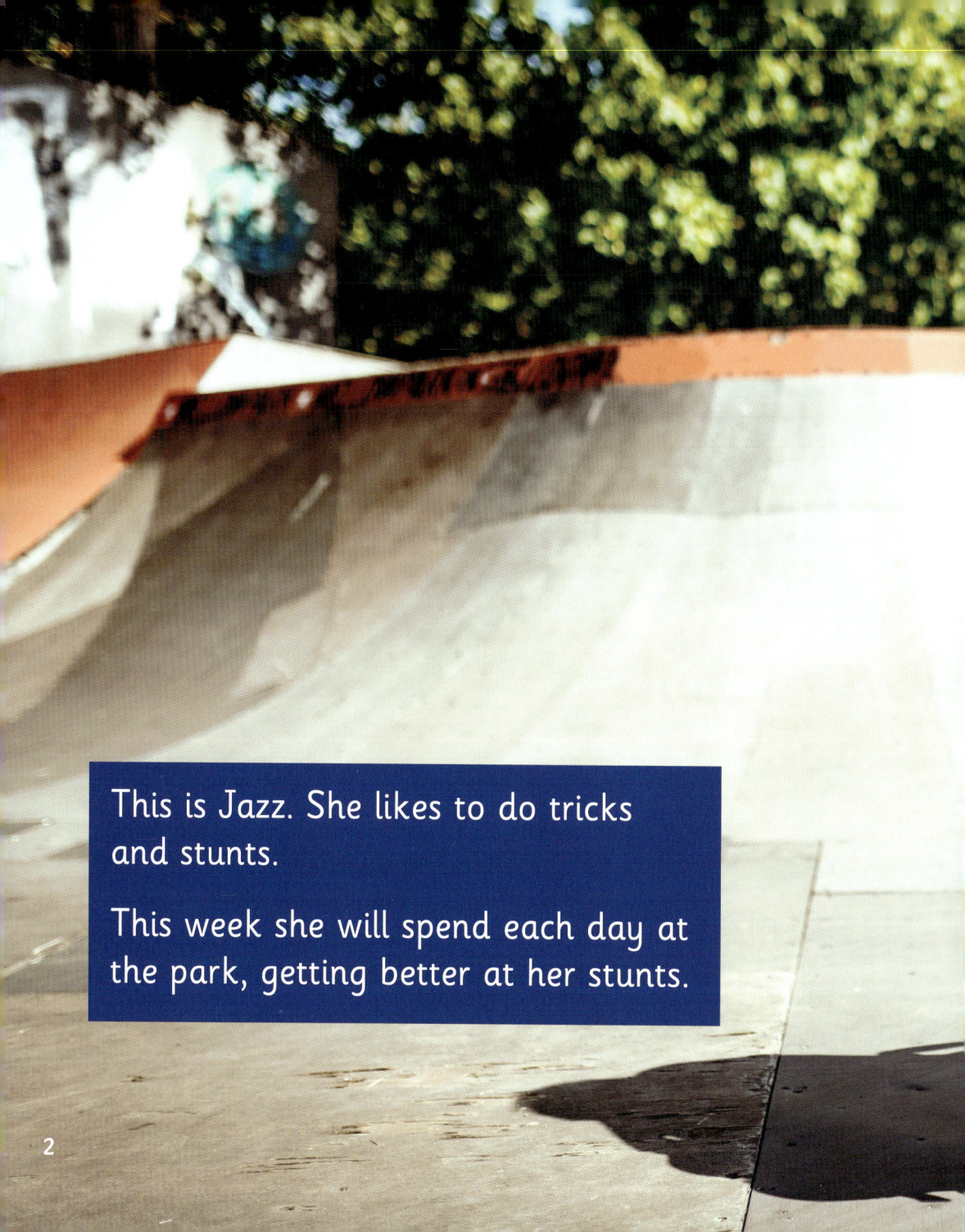

This is Jazz. She likes to do tricks and stunts.

This week she will spend each day at the park, getting better at her stunts.

She has pads and a helmet, so she will not get hurt if the chair tips up.

It's important to have the right kit.

On Tuesday, there is no one at the park, apart from Jazz.

So she plays on the short ramps.

On Wednesday, she zooms down all the short ramps with no problems.

Jazz is proud of what she can do. It's a thrilling feat.

On Thursday, she has fun doing tricks on her hands.

She can tilt the chair, then spin and twist it around.

She needs strong arms and hands to do such tricks.

On Friday, Jazz looks at the top ramp.

It's the highest ramp in the park. It's steep too. That's a big drop from the top!

This high ramp will be a big test for Jazz.

When will she go from this top ramp?

Not yet! Not now! She will wait a day.

On Saturday, Jazz is back at the top of the highest ramp.

Now she will go down.

She shoots down from the top like a rocket! Oh, Jazz! That is so quick!

What a thrill to speed down from the top. She feels as if she will sprout wings!

On Sunday, there are lots of stunt fans in the park. They are all looking to get their fun and thrills too.

So, on Sunday, Jazz has a rest!

This week, Jazz tried her best. She didn't crash at all.

Is there no limit to the stunts she can do?

Jazz is confident she can be a big stunt star.